This book belongs to:

....

....

For Terry and Vernon

A TEMPLAR BOOK

First published in the UK in 2022 by Templar Books,
an imprint of Bonnier Books UK
4th Floor, Victoria House,
Bloomsbury Square, London WC1B 4DA
Owned by Bonnier Books
Sveavägen 56, Stockholm, Sweden
www.bonnierbooks.co.uk

Text and illustration copyright © 2022 by Duncan Beedie
Design copyright © 2022 by Templar Books

1 3 5 7 9 10 8 6 4 2

ISBN 978-1-78741-986-5

This book was typeset in Clarendon
The illustrations were created digitally

Edited by Alison Ritchie
Designed by Genevieve Webster
Production by Ché Creasey

Printed in China

templar
books

NO SLEEP FOR BEAR

DUNCAN BEEDIE

Bear stood outside his cave and breathed in the chilly air.
The leaves on the trees had turned red. Winter was coming,
and Bear was looking forward to a very long sleep . . .

A **very** long sleep indeed.

Bear made a list:

Tummy full – TICK.

Blanket fluffy – TICK.

Cave cosy – TICK.

He gently closed his eyes,

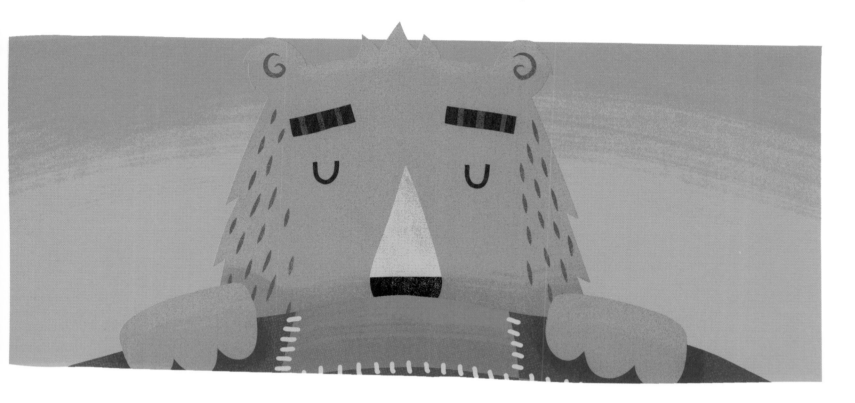

but . . .

He could **not** sleep.

Oh dear! thought Bear.
It's nearly winter and I must go to sleep.

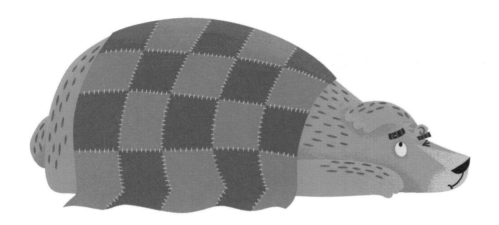

He tossed and he turned . . .

until the birds started chirping.

It was **morning!**

Bear decided a nice long walk might tire him out.
He walked until the sun began to set.

Just then he saw Blackbird chirping away at the top
of a tree, before settling down in his nest to sleep.

Maybe that will work for me? thought Bear.

He climbed to the top of the tallest tree and began singing:

GRROOWWOO!

The branch was uncomfortable on Bear's bottom.

He fidgeted and he fussed until the sky turned pink.

It was morning **again!**

That day, Bear walked even further.

He saw Badger burrowing into his sett for a snooze.

Perhaps a cosy underground burrow is what I need?
thought Bear.

But Badger's sett was
scarcely big enough for Bear,
let alone both of them.

He felt an icy cold wind
blast his toes. He squished
and he squashed until
he felt his feet gradually
warm in the sun.

It was morning
once again!

Back in his cave, Bear was writing another list when Bat fluttered in and hung upside-down from the ceiling.

nice long walk X
sing like
blackbird X
burrow with
Badger   X

That might be worth a try, thought Bear. So he gripped
the cave roof with his feet and hung upside-down too.
He swooned and he swayed until he fell to the ground.

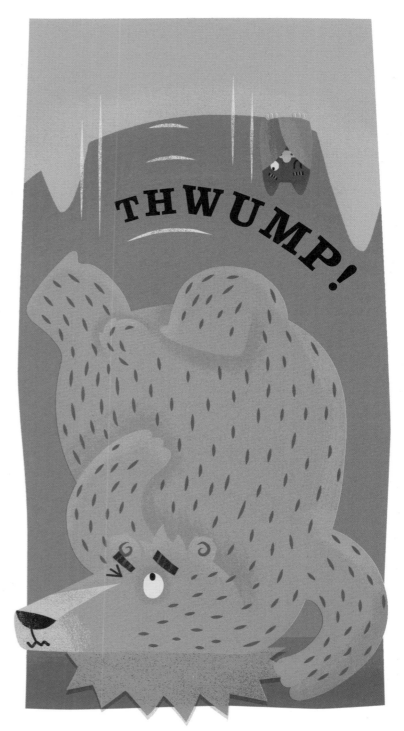

THWUMP!

This is never going to work, thought Bear as he plodded
out into the night.

The moon was shining brightly as Bear
crept through the forest towards the pond.

He found Frog sitting on a log.
"Trouble sleeping?" croaked Frog,
opening one goggly eye.

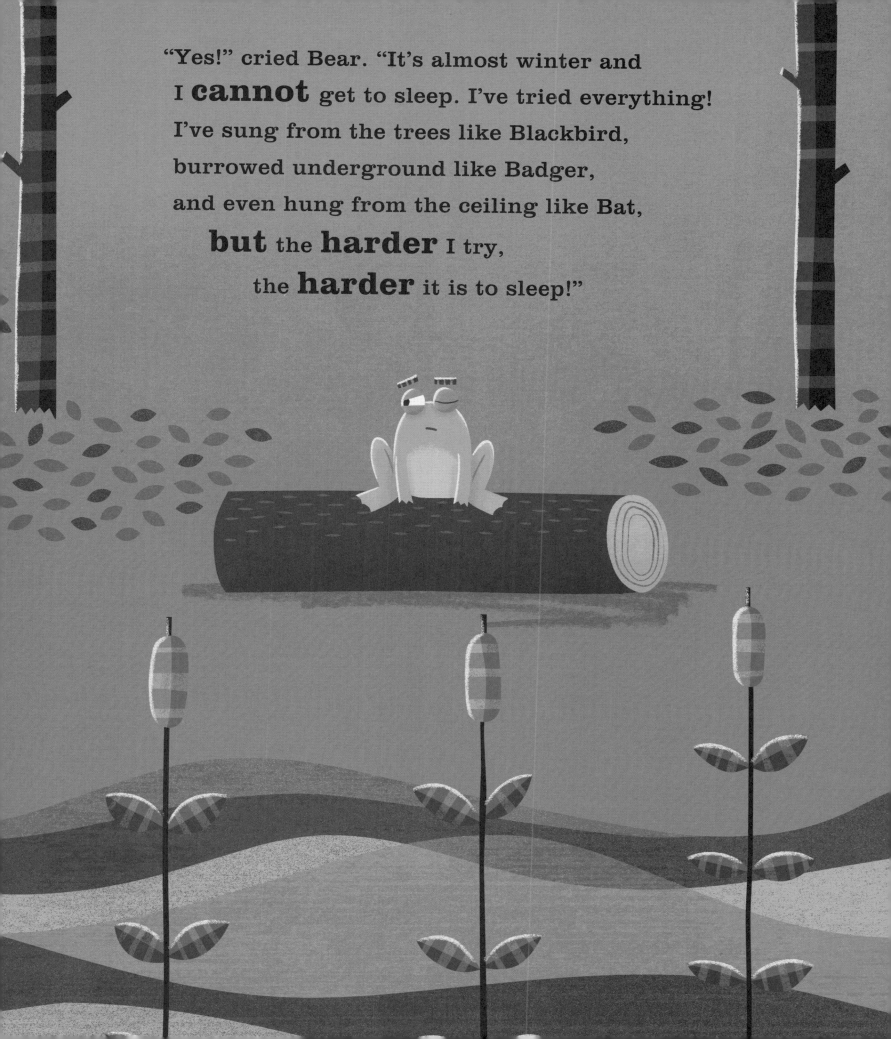

"Yes!" cried Bear. "It's almost winter and
I **cannot** get to sleep. I've tried everything!
I've sung from the trees like Blackbird,
burrowed underground like Badger,
and even hung from the ceiling like Bat,
but the **harder** I try,
the **harder** it is to sleep!"

"It sounds to me like you're trying too hard," Frog said.

"So hard, in fact, that you've forgotten the most important thing."

"What's that?" asked Bear.

"You've got to relax!" answered Frog. "Just copy me."

Frog sat.
Quiet and still.
Like a shiny
green pebble.

Bear sat still too, surrounded by the dark.
A cluster of fireflies hovered over the pond.
They looked like beautiful green stars.

Lip-lap, lip-lap went the water at the pond's edge.
Bear's tummy went up and down as he breathed
in time to the sound.

Lip . . . . . lap . . . . . lip . . . . . lap . . . . .

Bear's head felt heavy . . . his eyelids started to droop . . .

And then he fell . . .

. . . asleep.

His loud snoring woke up the **whole** forest.

"We've **got** to get Bear back into his cave,
or none of us will get any sleep," the animals gasped.

So they heaved and they huffed,

and they pushed and they puffed,

through deep drifts and whipping winds.

The journey took them **all** winter.

Bear was finally back in his cave,

just as the first buds of spring were sprouting.

Bear opened his eyes and had a great big STR-E-E-ETCH.

He started a new list for all the fun things he would do
now that his long sleep was over.

picnic

scratching

dress up
with Frog

Singing lessons
with Blackbird

roller skating

hide &
Seek

tennis
with Badger

acro-bat-ics
with Bat

book club
with Worm

more
picnics

But it looked like the fun would have to wait
just a little bit longer.

THE END